DOLPHIN

FAST

ARMADILLO

SLOW

FOX

FAST

TIGER

FAST

KOALA

SLOW

OSTRICH

FAST

HEDGEHOG

SLOW

TORTOISE

SLOW

Snail Boy is dedicated to King Berlew—
my honorable lawyer, great friend,
and protector of Snail Boy.

First edition 2003

Library of Congress Cataloging-in-Publication Data

McGuirk, Leslie.
Snail Boy / by Leslie McGuirk. — 1st ed.
p.   cm.
Summary: A snail the size of a pony, afraid that he will
wind up in a circus, or worse, sets out to become someone's pet.
ISBN 0-7636-1259-6
[1. Snails—Fiction. 2. Pets—Fiction.] I. Title.
PZ7.M17752 Sn 2003
[E]—dc21   2002067058

2 4 6 8 10 9 7 5 3 1

Printed in Hong Kong

This book was typeset in Gararond Medium.
The illustrations were done in ink and gouache.

Candlewick Press
2067 Massachusetts Avenue
Cambridge, Massachusetts 02140

visit us at www.candlewick.com

Snail Boy

Leslie McGuirk

CANDLEWICK PRESS
CAMBRIDGE, MASSACHUSETTS

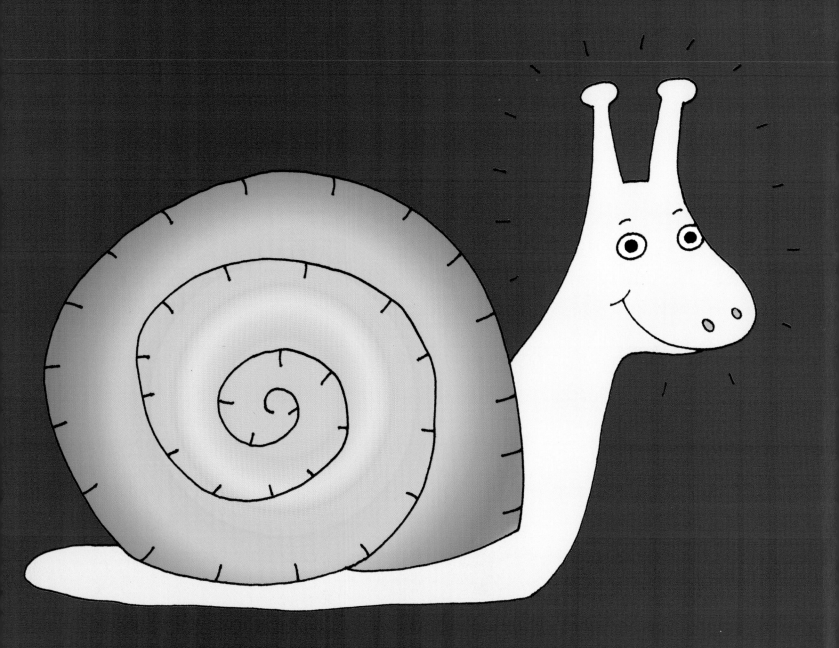

This is Snail.

He is a Gigantic Exotic Gastropod in full bloom.

He is, in fact, as big as this pony.

Snail is extremely rare, so he hides most of the day.

He's afraid the wrong kind of person, like a Snail Hunter, will catch him.

At night he sleeps in his secret hiding place
and has bad dreams.

One morning, Snail woke up and had a lifesaving idea.

He needed to find just the right owner.

He began his search at the local park. He climbed a giant tree and looked down at his prospects.

There was one boy—a boy with a red cap— who was playing all by himself.

"I'll ask him," said Snail, "because he's alone, like me."

Snail crawled back down to the ground.
He waited inside his shell.

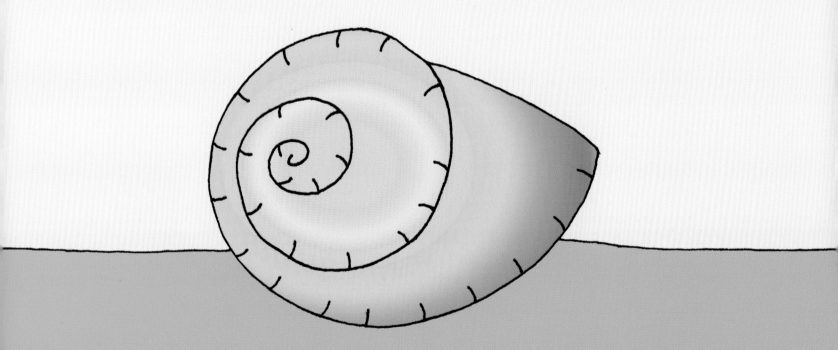

When the boy ran past, Snail popped out and said, "Do you have the time . . ."

But before Snail could finish his question, the boy screamed.

"You scared me," said the boy. "You're as big as a pony!"

"Yes," said Snail, "but I'm better looking, and much more interesting. Do you have time to take care of a pet like me?"

The boy laughed. "Are you kidding? You're just a giant slowpoke. If you were a cheetah, I might be interested."

"Cheetah-schmeetah!" pooh-poohed Snail.

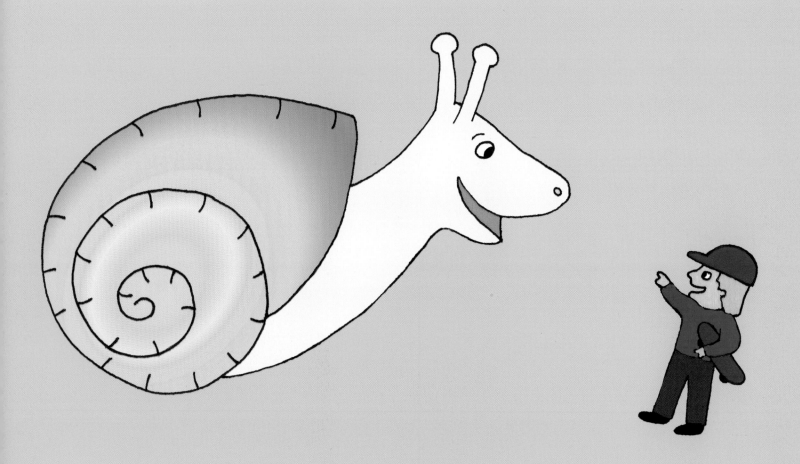

"Those fast pets just leave you in the dust.
I won't leave you in the dust or anyplace else!
Plus, you never need to groom me."

"Can you do tricks?" asked the boy.

"Of course! Watch me," said Snail.

Snail shook his whole body.

"What was that?" asked the boy.

"SHAKE!" answered Snail with pride.
The boy laughed.

"Now watch this," said Snail, and he showed
the boy the rest of his tricks.

ROLL OVER!

PLAY DEAD!

"I think talking is my best trick of all,
though, don't you?" Snail asked.

"Definitely," said the boy. "Too bad I'm still
not really looking for a pet."

"Oh well," said Snail. "I was just imagining how good you would look, up on my back."

"You mean I could ride you?" asked the boy.

"Normally only licensed snail operators can ride me, but if you were my owner . . ."

"All right!" said the boy. "I'll be your owner!"

"Great!" said Snail. "Hop on. You are now my official Snail Boy."

And slowly, slowly they made their way to the pet store.

Together they picked out a collar, food dishes, snail chow, and some toys.

When they passed the hamster display,
the boy told them all, "The snail's mine!"

As they left the store, it started to rain.

"We're going to get wet," announced Snail Boy.

"Let's go inside my shell," said Snail.

Snail ducked in first.

The boy followed.

"It's nice and cozy in here, and really pink," said the boy.

"I'm glad you like it," said Snail.

"This can be our own private clubhouse!" said the boy. They both thought this was an excellent idea.

They talked for a long time, about what they wanted to be when they grew up and what they were going to have for dinner. Then the rain stopped falling, and they climbed out.

"That was fun," said Snail Boy.
"I'm really lucky you're my pet."

Snail replied with a word that sounded like a backwards hiccup.

"You just made a funny noise!" laughed Snail Boy.

"That's what snails say to each other when they're happy," said Snail.

"If you're happy now," said Snail Boy, "just wait until you see my trampoline." And off they went.

WORM

SLOW

GAZELLE

FAST

SLOTH

SLOW

CHEETAH

FAST

MANATEE

SLOW

FISH

FAST

PANDA

SLOW

HUMMINGBIRD

FAST